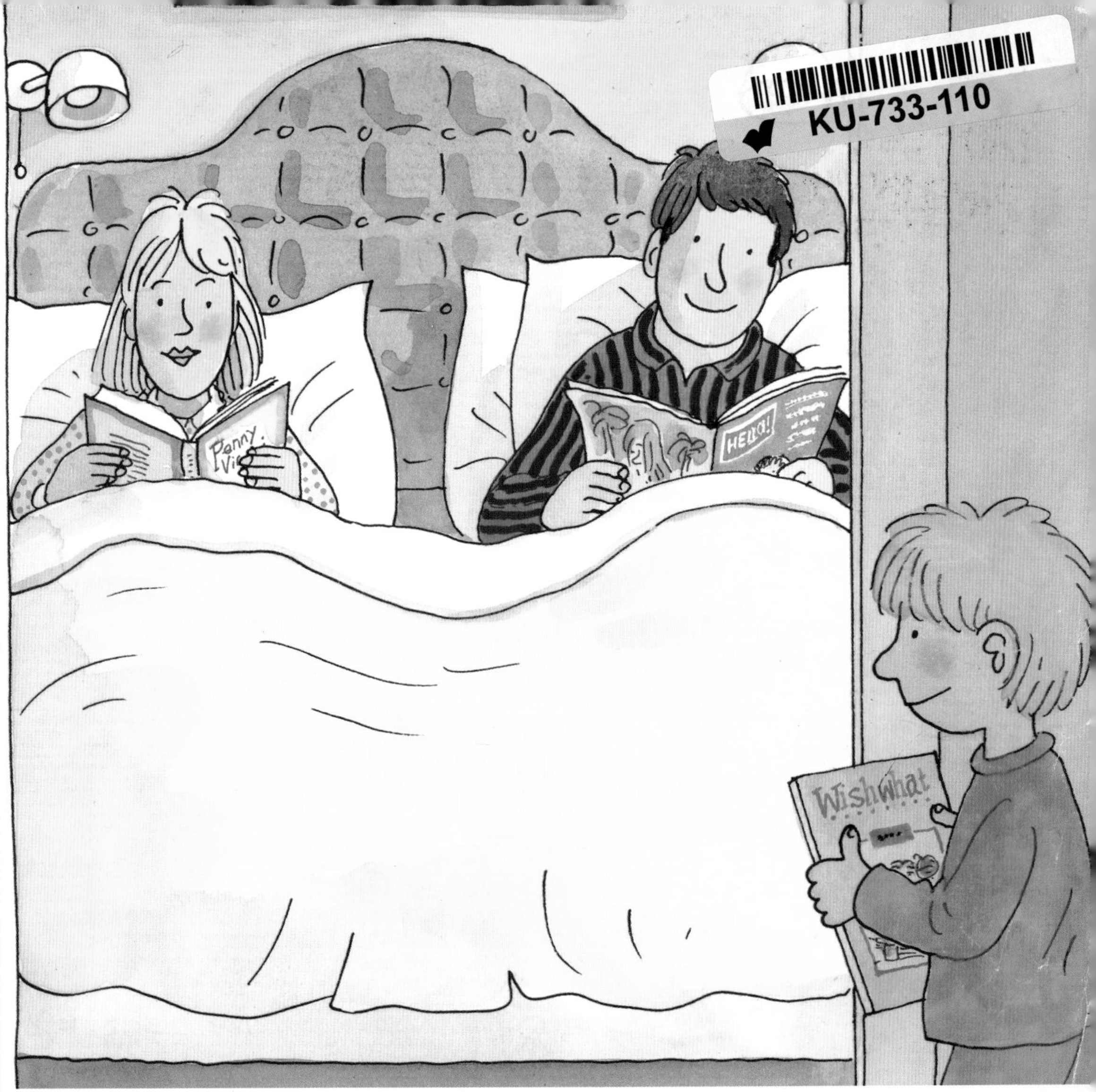

Mum and Dad.

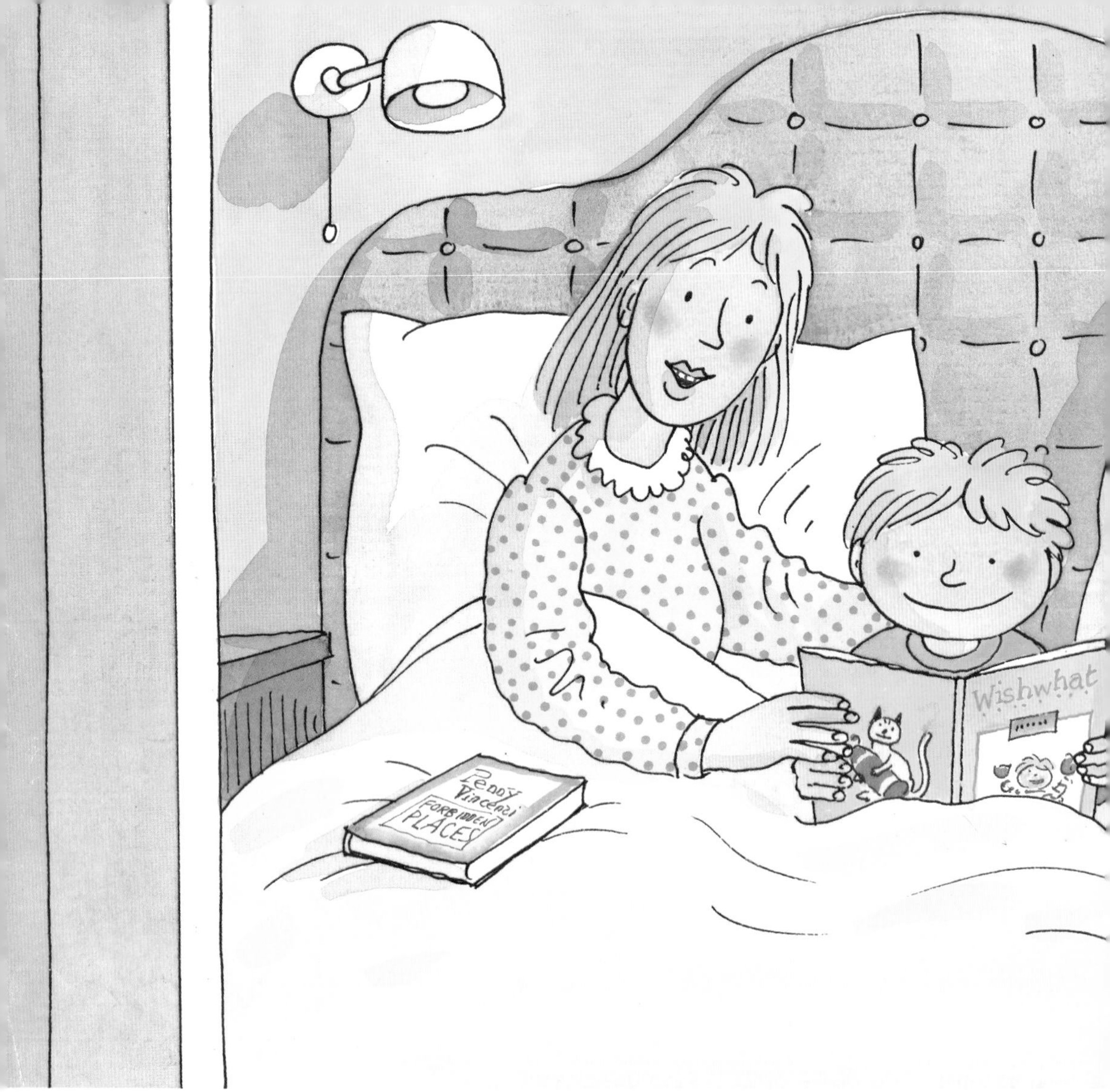

Mum, Kipper and Dad.

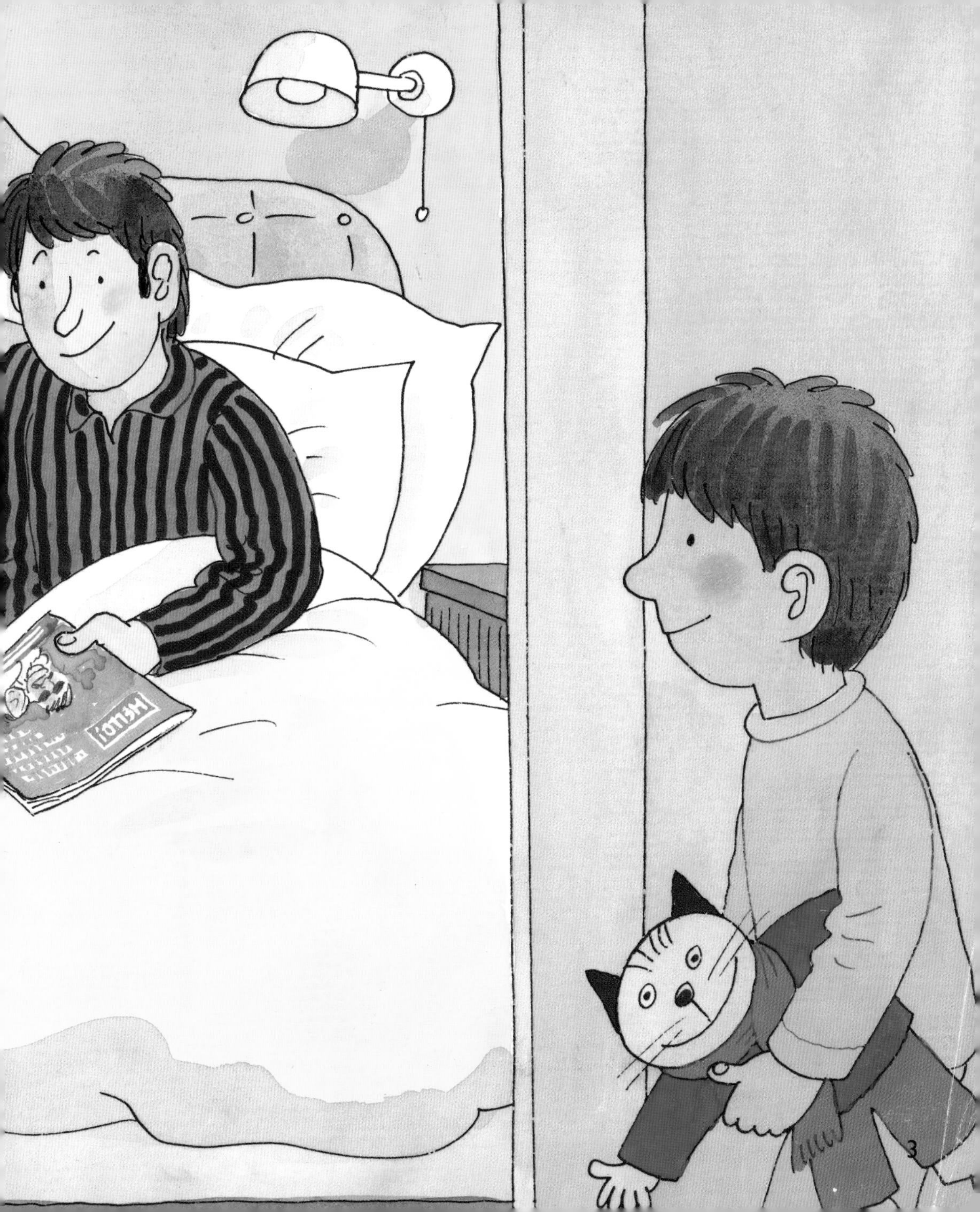

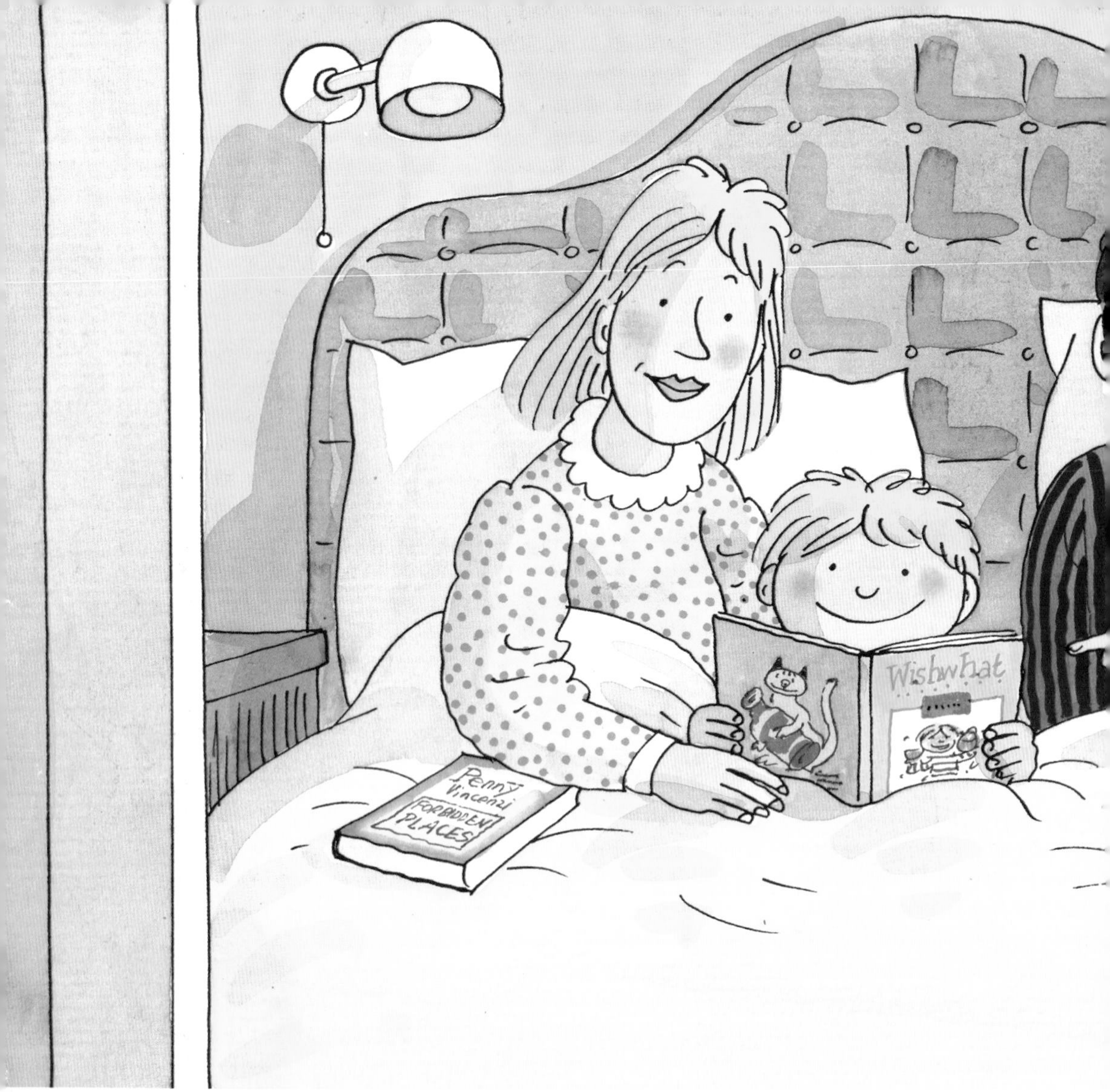

Mum, Kipper, Dad and Chip.

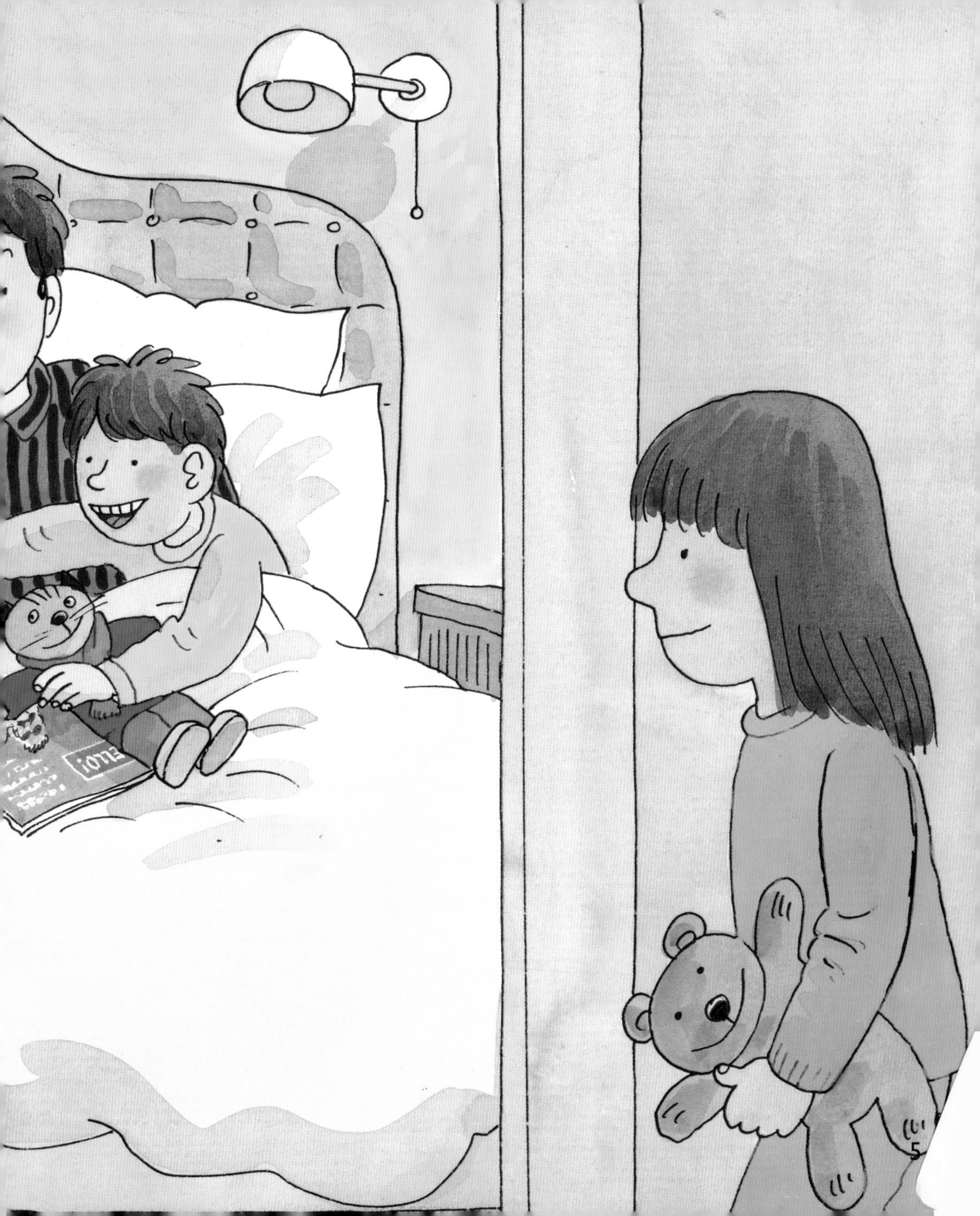

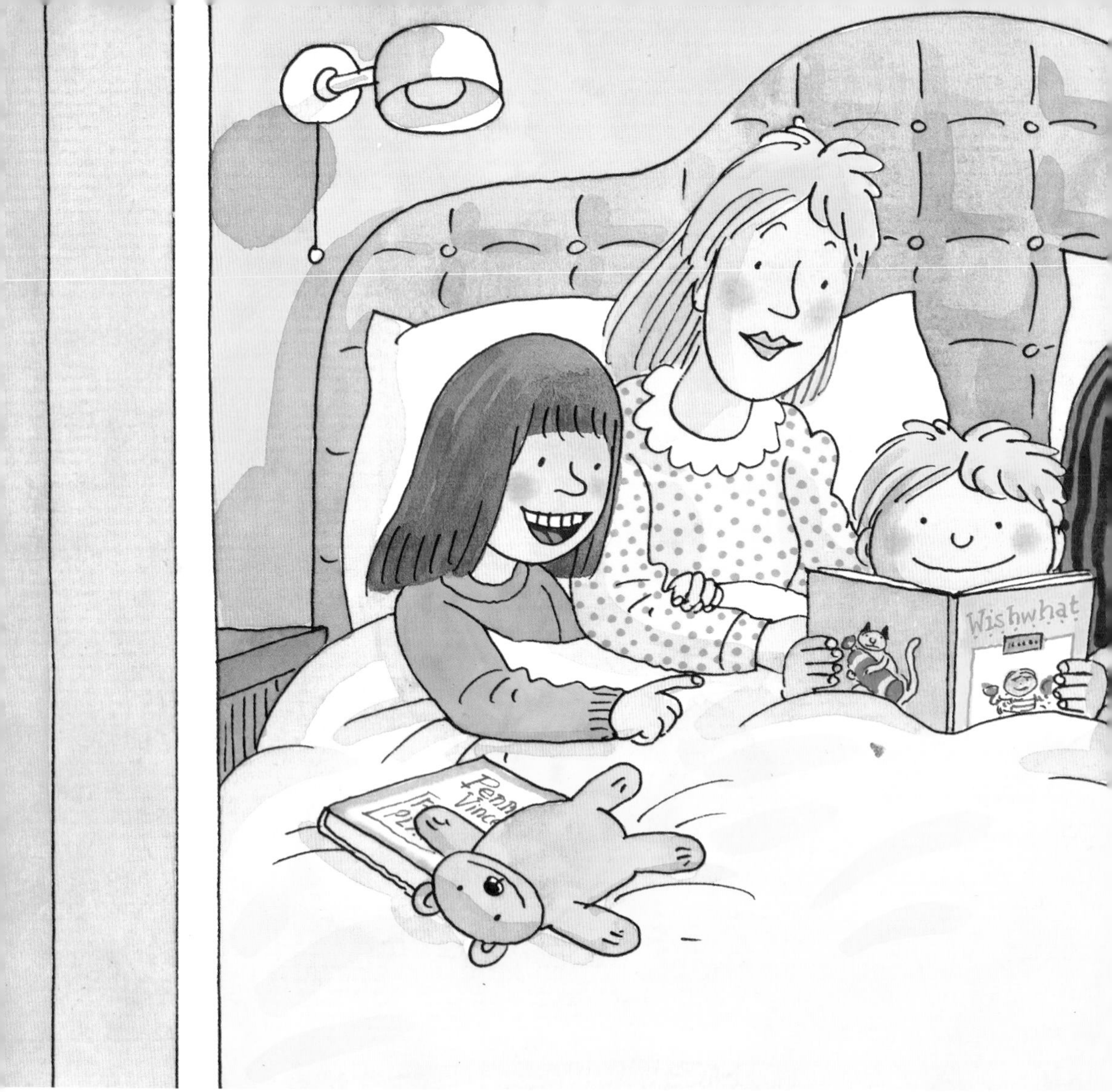

Biff, Mum, Kipper, Dad, Chip,

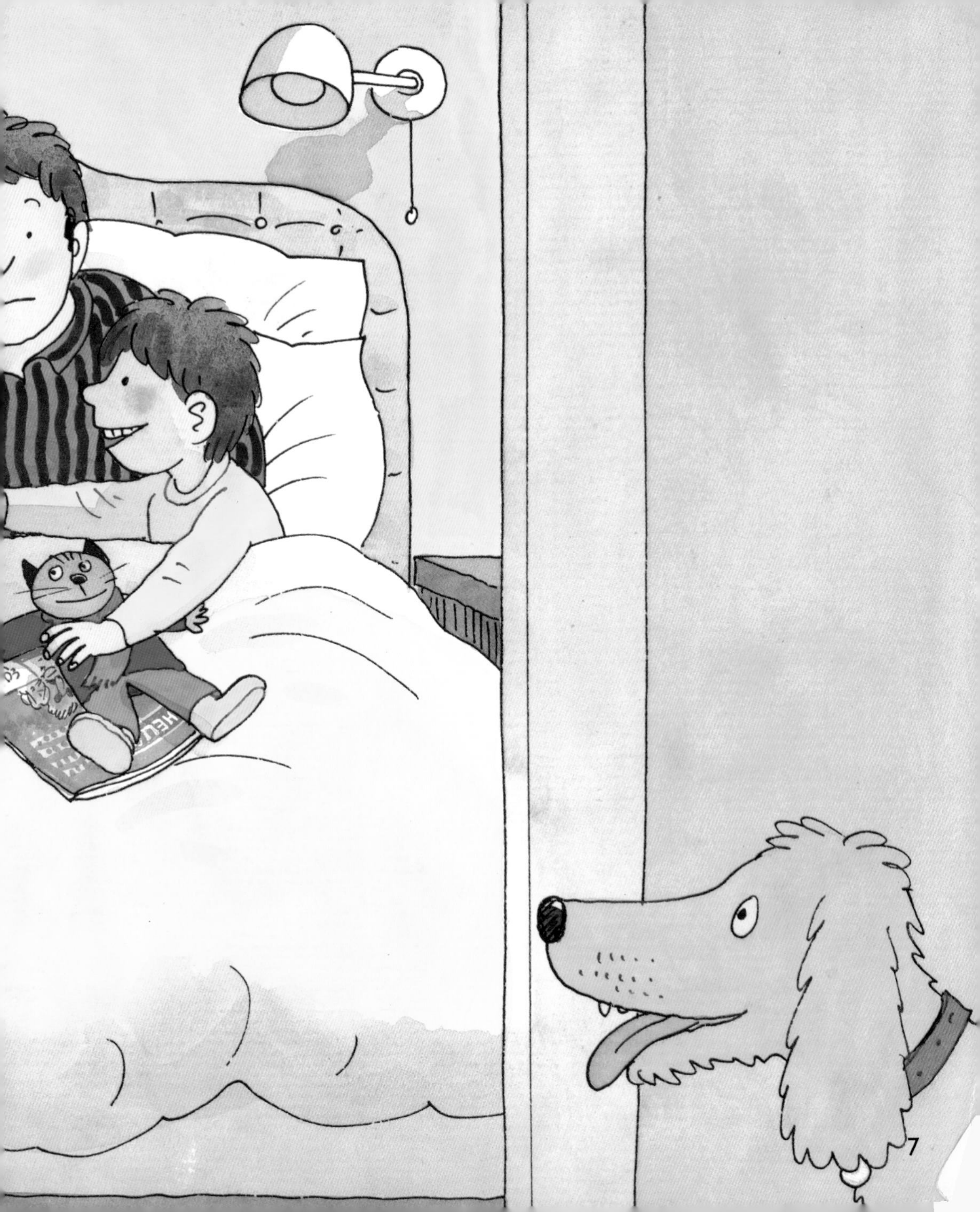

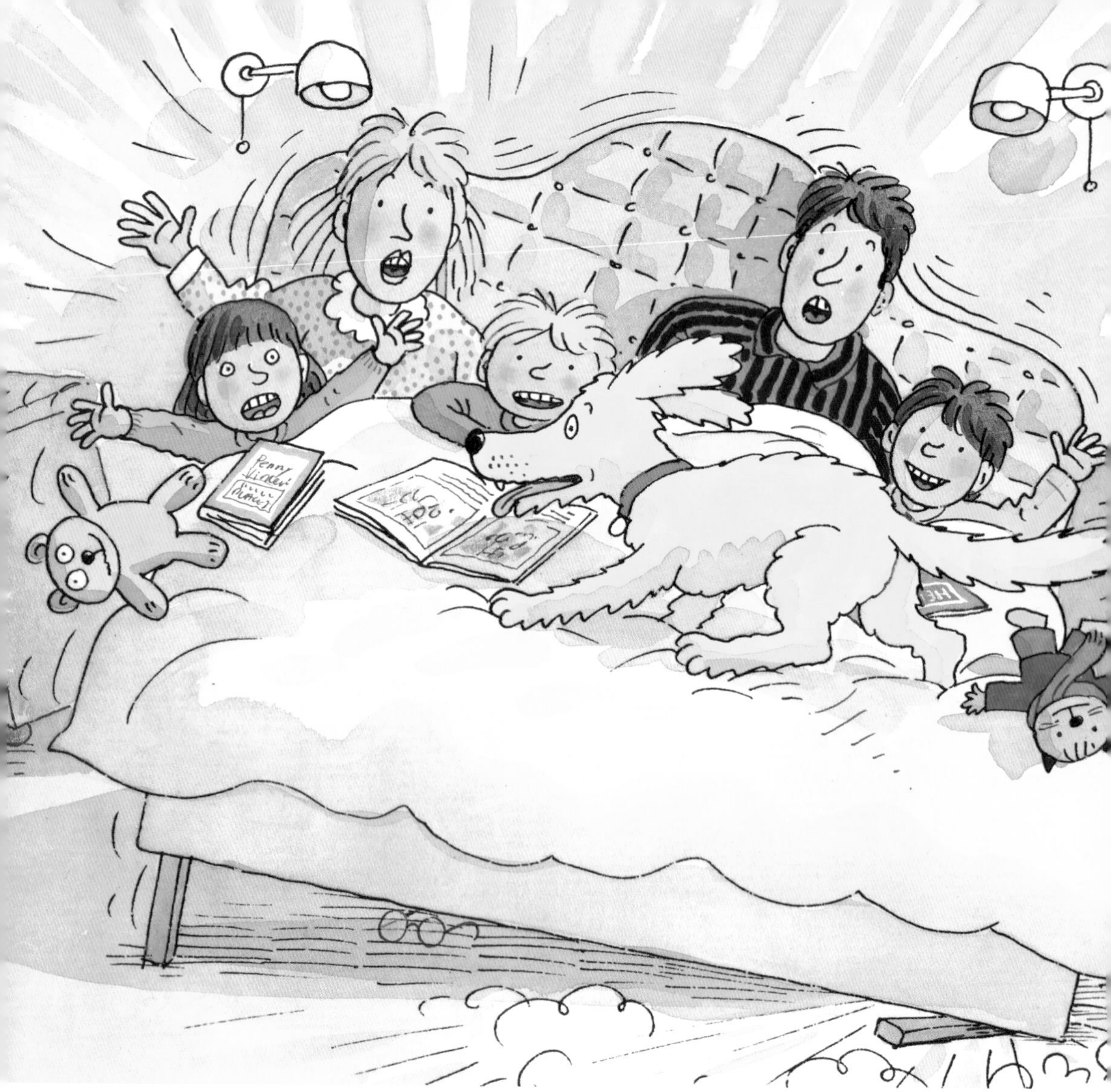

and Floppy.